Clare's Naughty Girl

An MDLG and ABDL story of a lesbian Mistress who trains a brat to be Mommy's good girl

By Tina Moore

Table of Contents

Chapter 1

Clare had been focused, driven, and very alone for as long as she could remember, so it was not uncommon for her to be early to work. In fact, for as long as she could remember, she had been early for everything. Her attentive nature prevented her from ever being late, even when she had accidentally overslept one morning before work.

Today would be no different as she picked up a bagel on her way into the office. Clare had worked for a large accounting firm in the heart of the city for the past six years. During that time, she had quietly gone about her business, happily avoiding the office bullies who always had a new piece of gossip to share and popularity contests that reminded her of high school.

"I can't believe Stacey is wearing his ex-wife's necklace," Clare heard Holly gossip on the way down the corridor.

Holly was one of those women who stopped men in their tracks and who made wives jealous. She had the typical vogue look of full, bouncy blonde waves of hair which tumbled down her back. Her blue eyes looked like sapphires, and her soft pink lips were contrasted against her creamy white skin. She had a slender figure, one which often made Clare wonder why she was an accountant instead of a model. Clare, on the other hand, could be described as naturally beautiful. However, she was not painted with the same elixir as Holly. Clare maintained short manicured nails in a light shade of beige; her hair was a mahogany brown falling straight down her back, and her green eyes were nothing out of the ordinary.

"I know, the divorce isn't even settled yet, and he is already giving her stuff away to the next. What a jerk, and what a mole for actually accepting it. It's bad enough that they all work on the same floor, they don't need to rub it in her face," said one of Holly's minions.

Holly turned around to see Clare behind her and her friend Tracey.

"What do you think about it, then?" Holly asked Clare. Clare wishing she hadn't, turned and looked out the wall-length window, which gave a 180' view of the city.

"I don't think it's any of our business," Clare replied, being less than amused. Holly, unsatisfied with her answer, waved her hand dismissively.

"I knew you would say that," Holly stated, turning left at the end of the corridor, making Clare relieved she was going in the opposite direction.

Grateful that Friday night had finally arrived, Clare jumped out of the shower and looked at herself in the mirror. Her full double D breasts were going to look amazing in the leather bra and top she was planning on giving a whirl tonight. She pulled on her black leather pants and zipped up her matching boots as she put her hair up in a high, slicked-back ponytail and put her whip in her bag. She walked around her house topless as she made herself a drink and did her makeup. Dark smoky unforgiving eyes stared back at her as she applied a dark shade of red to her lips. Highlighting her cheekbones, she sipped her drink and began thinking of the fun the night would bring. She walked back into her bedroom and put on her new bra, and top enjoying the tight feeling of it against her toned body. Flicking through social media and chatting with a few girls online, Clare finished her drink but stayed chatting until the conversation became boring. Closing her laptop lid and taking one last look in the mirror as she grabbed her wallet and keys, she headed out the door.

She arrived at the party 3 hours after it had started. She didn't consider this late she considered this was making sure the party was in full swing by the time she got there. As she walked up to the warehouse, a sudden flash of blonde hair from the entrance caught her attention. Clare smiled, knowing that tonight would be fun. She had been looking forward to this party for weeks. The host was a close friend of hers, and she had explained that there would be different rooms for different types of kink. Clare was excited. Usually, she had to choose between attending to a Mommy Domme party or something more aligned with her strict, merciless Mistress side. Tonight she was hoping she could combine both.

Clare followed the blonde-haired woman into the party and was not disappointed. She made her way through the crowds of people. There was a large circular bar in the middle of the warehouse with topless slave girls and boys, which you could write a message on while you ordered. Although the warehouse was only one level, the way Clare's friend Sophie had sent up the rooms made it look unusually large. Clare ordered two shots of whiskey followed by a vodka lemonade chaser, grabbing her waitresses jaw and writing something obscene along her throat. Clare shot the whiskey and got up to mingle, running into a few people she knew along the way. As the music echoed through the warehouse, Clare found herself going from room to room. She had no interest in half of them, but she was thorough and didn't want to miss a thing. Leaving the puppy playpen behind, she made her way to the flogging stations and finished her drink as she watched a pretty girl be whipped by three people. Going into the next room, Clare smiled wickedly at what she saw. The feel of this room was unlike the others as Mommies and Daddies played with babies, sat around watching babies play, or were punishing their naughty little ones. But what made Clare's blood burn with desire was the baby playing by herself in the corner. Clare sat down and watched her. She was playing with a set of blocks, making a tower and then knocking it over, giggling to herself.

Clare got up and walked over to her, kneeling and enjoying the woman's surprised face.

"Hey Baby," Clare said sweetly, taking a block and putting it onto the blonde's tower. The baby was lost for words as she stared at Clare.

"What are you playing?" Clare asked.

"Blocks," the pink diapered baby replied, blushing slightly and looking down at the ground.

"Can I play too?" Clare said, smiling as the baby nodded her head.

"You're good at that Holly," Clare said as Holly pushed over the tower she and Clare had just built. Holly giggled and reached for Clare, who pulled her onto her lap.

"Does the baby like cuddles?" Clare said, cuddling Holly tight. Holly nodded and turned her head; a nervous look came across her face.

"Clare, you won't tell anyone about this, will you?" Holly asked fearfully. Clare liked seeing the most popular woman at work almost shake in fear in her arms. She took her time to reply, looking down and rubbing the front of Holly's thick diaper.

"Mm, I don't know," Clare said when she finally replied, making Holly hold her breath.

"Of course I'll keep it to myself, little baby. I wouldn't want to see those pretty eyes cry!" Clare said, feeling Holly's body settle into her arms.

"Thanks," Holly said, looking down, suddenly embarrassed to be seen like this by Clare. Holly had heard the stories about how Clare was weird and into all sorts of dark magic and stuff. Seeing her tonight, Holly knew that none of that was right she was as weird as she was.

The night carried on with Clare and Holly playing together before Clare kissed her on her forehead and went back into the flogging room and went to work on a slave's back. She was almost satisfied when the lights of the warehouse were turned on, and the music stopped suddenly.

"Oh, I hate how she does that," Clare said, referring to Sophie's method of ending a party. She rolled her eyes and began to walk out of the room and bumped into Holly, who had changed back into adult clothes. Clare took in her short schoolgirl skirt and white buttoned top, grabbing hold of her tie and pulling Holly towards her. Holly giggled and looked to the floor.

"The party is over, Clare," Holly said nervously as she looked down and kicked at the ground.

"For some," Clare replied, seductively reaching out and lifting Holly's head, so her eyes met hers. She leaned forward and whispered in Holly's ear as she ran her hand up and down her back. When Clare had finished talking, Holly nodded and followed her to her car, reaching for her hand, which made Clare excited. She liked to have girls need her, to want her to love them, and Holly's, take me now, attitude had always excited her.

"I'm interested to see your place," Holly said as Clare drove them to her house. Clare looked at Holly and placed her hand on Holly's thigh, caressing it gently.

"Show me," Clare said in a low voice, taking Holly's hand and pulling it towards the top of her skirt. Holly giggled as she began to play with herself. Clare bit her bottom lip as Holly's giggles turned to moans, and she watched as Holly came in her passenger seat.

"Did I say you could come?" Clare asked as she pulled into her driveway. Holly looked at Clare apologetically.

"That won't work on me pretty baby," Clare stated bluntly. She unlocked her front door and pulled Holly inside by her schoolgirl tie.

"Strip," Clare ordered over her shoulder as she made her way into her bedroom. Holly was unsure of where exactly Clare wanted her, so she took her clothes off and waited for Clare to return. When Clare came back, she was topless and holding a baby blanket. Holly's eyes were wide, and her heart was racing.

"Come and cuddle Mommy Holly," Clare instructed, sitting on the couch and waiting for Holly to join her. Holly's naked body felt cold as Clare wrapped her in the blanket.

"Now, tell Mommy what kind of things you like sweetie. Let me know all your dirty little secrets," Clare said, beginning to stroke Holly's arm up and down. Clare had whispered in Holly's ear the things she had wanted to do to her, but she always wanted to know what her playmates wanted as well. Mostly, Clare just liked to use it as leverage to push a limit slightly.

"In like sex or with general age play?" Holly replied, seeking clarification. Clare kissed her forehead.

"Both," she bluntly said.

"Well, in sex I like being penetrated, my clit is kinda useless, and I don't feel much. I like anal but not being fisted there. I like being spanked but not whipped or canned, and I like being gagged with anything except for feet." Holly thought for a moment before continuing.

"I like being tied up, but I don't really like being hurt too much. And age play stuff, I am pretty general. I like cuddles and Mommy time and diapers, and I love playing with building blocks," Holly explained. Clare had given Holly her undivided attention and enjoyed watching as Holly lit up when talked about what she liked as a baby. *So, she'll let me fuck her, but it's love she's really after,* Clare thought to herself, noticing the animated way Holly spoke.

"What do you like?" Holly asked Clare. She moved Holly onto her breast and made her suck her nipple while she replied.

"As a general, I like spanking naughty girls firmly. I like dressing them in leather while they are in their diapers, and I like to mercilessly use them as pretty little fuck-dolls. I think I might be too rough for you, sweetheart. I love treating my little girl like a princess, but I thoroughly enjoy disciplining her. Clare moved Holly to her other breast and lovingly stroked her hair.

"We could still try Mommy, though," Holly said around Clare's breast. Clare looked down at Holly, who was happily sucking and licking her nipple.

"Oh yeah, I'm going to let you try," Clare agreed, taking Holly's hand and leading her to the floor. She went back into her room, and when she came out again, she was jerking her leather harnessed strap-on.

"You don't look like a little girl anymore, Holly; you look like a little slut, so I'm going to fuck you like one. Kneel," Clare instructed. Holly knelt before her and Clare slapped her cheek with her cock before pushing it past Holly's lips and down her throat, making her gag instantly.

"Swallow," Clare commanded, ramming her cock further down Holly's throat, smiling as tears rolled down her face. Holly's saliva dripped from around Clare's cock and onto her tits, which delighted Clare. She bent down slightly and pulled hard on Holly's nipples making her open her mouth wider as she yelped in pain. Clare took the opportunity to force her thick cock deeper into Holly's mouth and would pull on her nipples when she felt like Holly's mouth wasn't full enough. Clare roughly fucked Holly's mouth until Holly couldn't feel her jaw and had given up trying to push Clare away, instead she had taken it like the fuck-doll Clare was using her as.

"Here," Clare said, taking her cock out of Holly's mouth and snapping her fingers towards the floor. Holly lay down on her back on Clare's living room floor, and Clare went to her bedroom once more. This time when she came out, Clare carried a big teddy bear, a pacifier, and another blanket. She pulled Holly to her feet and held her as she put the teddy bear on the floor, the blanket over the top, and pushed Holly back down next. Clare wrapped the blanket around Holly and rubbed the pacifier over her spit covered cock before pushing it gently into Holly's mouth. Clare grabbed her hips and turned her over, so Holly was laying tummy down on top of the adult-sized teddy bear. She lifted Holly's hips and rubbed her cock up and down her wet slit before using the tip of the cock to part them.

"Pretty baby," Clare said, slapping Holly's left ass cheek.

"I'm going to spank this slutty little ass until you let me in, do you understand?" Clare explained. Holly nodded her head as Clare came down on her right ass cheek, making her bottom jiggle. Clare grabbed two big handfuls of Holly's bubble butt and pushed herself into her pussy, spanking her left cheek again when she was still not inside of Holly. Holly moaned and wriggled under Clare's touch, getting wetter and wetter as Clare spanked her. Clare grabbed Holly's reddening ass after a series of spanks and pushed against her pussy again, feeling Holly's submission.

Just as an hour passed, Holly gave in, falling limp on the teddy, which was now covered in her cum, and Clare finally filled her with her cock, making Holly cry out but not refuse her.

"Did you think I'd give up little girl?" Clare asked as she powerfully thrust into Holly's pussy, making her gasp each time Clare filled her. Holly just nodded.

"I thought I could outlast you," she said breathlessly through moans and gasps. Clare laughed as she pounded Holly's pussy.

"Outlast, Mommy? I don't think so," Clare replied, feeling Holly close to cumming. Holly felt it too as she clenched her pussy and released feeling the warm liquid of her squirting cunt drip out from around Clare's cock. Impressed with herself, Clare kept her cock inside of Holly, who wriggled uncomfortably underneath her.

"What's the magic word, baby?" Clare prompted knowing that Holly had had enough.

"Please," Holly said breathlessly.

"Please, Mommy," Clare said, ramming her again, making her squeal.

"Please, Mommy," Holly half begged and sighed with relief, happy to feel Clare gently pull out of her. Holly shuddered as the aftershock of her intense orgasm hit her, and her pussy leaked cum onto the teddy bears thigh. Clare smiled and took off her cock. She laid down next to Holly, who weakly smiled at her, completely spent and laying in her cum.

"Shower and bed, little one?" Clare asked, nodding Holly. She took Holly's hand and gently lifted her, holding her lovingly as Holly adjusted to standing. Clare led her to the bathroom, where she ran a warm shower and took off her pants. She pushed Holly under the water and watched as Holly began to wash. Clare enjoyed the surprised look on Holly's face when she turned around, and Holly saw her back piece.

"I didn't know your whole back was tattooed," she said in amazement. Clare just raised an eyebrow and got into the shower with Holly.

"I want you gone by morning, little one," Clare said, pulling Holly in for a cuddle. Although she was kicking her out, she still wanted Holly to be alright with it.

"Yeah, sure. Clare?" Holly asked Clare, who was shaking her head.

"Mommy," Clare corrected to a nodding Holly, who looked down at her feet. The water felt nice on her spanked red ass, and Clare noticed a bratty smile come across her face.

"Mommy. My bottom doesn't even feel sore anymore. Guess you're not as tough as you think you are," Holly teased. Clare smirked, and before Holly could say another word, Clare had Holly's neck firmly in her grip and had taken off the showerhead from its mounted position. She flicked the cold water down and held the showerhead right onto Holly's freshly fucked cunt. Holly squirmed and squealed as Clare remained plain-faced as she let the warmer water run onto Holly's sensitive skin.

"Do you still want to play stupid little games with me, baby girl?" Clare said after two minutes. Holly shook her head.

"I can't hear you, baby," Clare replied to Holly's response.

"No, Mommy!" Holly half yelled, desperate to have the high pressured warm water off her aching pussy. Clare kept the showerhead on Holly for another minute before taking it away and pushing her down onto the shower floor. Clare got out of the shower and went to the cupboard. She took out a jar of expensive lotion and threw it into the shower at Holly.

"Don't fuck with Mommy Holly; it'll never end well for you," Clare instructed bluntly as she left the bathroom and turned the light off behind her.

Chapter 2

Clare was on a high all weekend as she replayed her evening with Holly. It had felt good to blow off some steam from the work week. She was all smiles as she dressed in her high-end business attire. A section of her cupboard that felt more like drag. In these clothes, Clare felt the collar and leash of her bosses. In her leather pants and whip, she felt like herself. *Everyone's someone's bitch*, Clare thought as she entered her office. Clare had made her way up to the sixth floor of the ten-story building but was more than interested in making it to the top. If her progress on her ten-year plan was anything to go by, she was right on track. Looking out her office window into the building, she saw Holly walk up the corridor. Holly turned her head and smiled meekly at Clare as she passed, causing Clare to sigh in contented bliss as she got back to the pile of paperwork which had made its way to her desk. But true to form, Holly had converted back to her bratty, self-righteous ways come lunchtime and was swaying her hips as she walked back down the corridor.

"Good afternoon Mr. Haze," she said as she passed one of the partners in her high pitched. I'm ready to be bent over and used as a cum dumpster type of manner. Clare watched as she looked into her office and gave a small victorious huff and walked away.

"And then, you'll never guess who I saw. I was coming out of Barry's Bar, and there she was, full leather, a dominatrix with this dude with a pink collar standing next to her. She must have been to some fancy dress party or something I had thought, but then he knelt on the dirty sidewalk and sat at her feet while she halted a taxi. It was so weird," Holly said, telling her friends a story over lunch. Clare had been sitting on the other side of the large potted plants and had heard the whole conversation. How, when Holly's friends had asked her what she did on the weekend she had made up a complete lie. Clare would have been fine with Holly lying about what she did. But it was that she had lied about what Clare had done that had made her blood boil. *As if I would be caught dead with a gimp boy at my feet,* Clare thought as she angrily ate her salad as Holly and her friends laughed at the lies Holly was telling them. The last thing Clare wanted was this little bitch ruining her chance of a final promotion. She knew this would spread around the office like wild-fire, so she took the rest of the day off.

Hurt, Clare took the long way home. She walked past her favorite shops but didn't feel like going it. *Why would she feel like she needed to lie about anything? Why not tell them what she did on the weekend?* Clare thought to herself as she kicked a stone onto the road. Her sadness turned to anger by the time she got home, and she slammed the door shut to her apartment. *If she's there tonight, I am going to fucking break her,* Clare thought to herself as she got ready to go to a kinkster meet and greet evening at one of her favorite bars. She wore her hair down tonight; it was not the scene where dress protocol was enforced. So she pulled on a smart pair of fitted black pants and an elegant red chiffon blouse matched with cream pumps. She wore a black fitted leather jacket over the top and a stare that could cut glass. Clare was still fuming from hearing Holly spread lies about her through the workplace, and she was grateful none of her colleagues had her phone number. The last thing she wanted to do was get into a who did what and who said what over Holly's little games.

Parking, Clare got out of her car and walked into the bar. She mingled with the usual people, slightly disappointed but slightly relieved that Holly wasn't there. As the night passed, Clare met several women she would have usually been happy to spend time with, and yet, tonight, they seemed dull. She excused herself from the girl she had been talking to for the better part of an hour and decided to go home. She exited the bar and turned the corner to see Holly walking in the opposite direction. Smiling widely, Holly sped up to catch Clare, who stopped walking and waited for Holly to reach her.

"Hi!" Holly exclaimed excitedly as she approached Clare. Clare just grabbed her by the wrist and firmly pulled her to the car.

"Hey, I wanted to go to the bar," Holly said as Clare unlocked her car. Clare looked at Holly with fire in her eyes.

"Get in," she roughly ordered. Holly made a pouty face and got into the car without a word. Clare went around to the driver's side and pulled out onto the street.

"Take off your panties," Clare ordered. Holly lifted her skirt almost without thinking and pulled them off.

"Play with your pussy, it'll be the only action it gets tonight," Clare explained. Holly reached down and began to stroke her clit.

"Keep your skirt up, baby," Clare said in the kindest tone she had used with Holly knowing that she wanted to fuck with her mind tonight.

Mommy, can I please cum?" Holly begged. Clare pulled into her driveway and pushed Holly's hand out-of-the-way and pulled her skirt down.

"No, that's Enough. Come, baby," Clare said, unbuckling Holly's seat belt. Holly got out and followed Clare into her house. This time Holly made it further than the living room as Clare took her into the bathroom straight away. She brought Holly to the bathroom counter and took a cake of soap out of her bathroom drawer and pushed it into Holly's mouth.

"Who the fuck do you think you are little one, making up lies about me," Clare angrily yelled as Holly struggled under her grip.

"I didn't," Holly tried to say, but the soap taste just intensified with her attempt to lie, so she shut up very quickly but continued to struggle.

"Don't even fucking try to tell me you didn't because I heard you, you little bitch," Clare added before taking out the cake of soap from her mouth. She ran the water for Holly, who lapped it up, eager to get the taste of soap out of her mouth.

"I'm sorry," Holly begged as she looked up at Clare, who was still furious. Clare didn't believe her, but there were still ways she could make sure Holly never lied about her again, and that was about to begin.

Clare took her out of the bathroom and into her bedroom. Holly looked around and took it all in. Clare's bedroom looked like a room from some vampire movie. It had high ceilings and a gothic style bed in the middle of the room. The candles illuminated dark linen Clare was lighting, which sat on marble shelves that wrapped around the room. On the floor was a thick fur rug, and there was a flogging cross in the corner facing the bed. Holly felt nervous.

"We are just still playing kinda safe, right, Mommy?" She asked as Clare took one of the candles and brought it over to the bed where Holly was sitting. Clare nodded, and Holly felt her energy shift. She knew Clare was going to give her a wonderful time; she just hoped she could handle it. Clare affectionately pushed Holly down and kissed her lovingly, enjoying feeling Holly's arms wrap around her, but Holly's shocked gasp broke their kiss as Clare poured candle wax onto her thigh.

"Shh, let Mommy show you some new things, baby," Clare said in a low, slightly depraved voice. Holly, who was still fully clothed, reached down to pull her skirt up, not wanting to get wax on it. Clare noticed and smiled.

"Oh, does the baby want her pretty clothes to stay nice and clean?" She said as she deliberately poured wax over Holly's skirt before lifting it and pouring the leftover wax onto her panties. Holly gasped and moaned as the warm wax stimulated her clit. Clare put the candle down on the concrete floor and looked down at her plaything.

"Don't worry, Mommy will get you some new clothes, baby girl," she said, slowly taking off Holly's ruined garments. Clare stood and took Holly's wrist firmly in her hand and pulled her over to the flogging cross. Clare's fingers were on Holly's pulse, and she felt her blood pump faster in her veins and laughed.

"I'm not going to hurt you, little girl," Clare reassured her as she tied both wrists high above her head. Clare stood back and saw Holly's elongated body. She pulled up her shirt and ran her fingernails over Holly's toned stomach, making her tense her muscles nervously.

"I guess you're going to stay there for Mommy until I'm

done with you. Isn't that right, baby?" Clare asked as she left the room. Ten minutes later, Holly was nervously sweating with the heat from the candles, and her nervousness and a trickle traced down her stomach, delighting Clare, who had returned.

"Don't you look divine and ready for the taking my pretty little doll," Clare said as she slapped Holly's thighs, making her part them. Clare never broke eye contact with Holly as she began to rub her gently. Holly broke and looked behind Clare to see what she had bought back into the room. A bondage rope lay sprawled across the bed next to shiny gold and white pacifier gag, and a vibrating butt plug.

"Are you going to tie me up?" Holly said breathlessly. It was hot in the room now, and Clare ran both her hands through Holly's hair, slicking it back as she kissed her neck.

"Yes, baby girl," Clare replied lovingly. Tonight, she was going to use Holly until she was nothing more than her good girl, knowing that she could stop at any time but refusing to. Clare took the gag, gently buckled it in place and rubbed Holly's pussy feeling how wet and eager she was. Clare was somewhat relieved Holly was still so willing to play and untied her from the cross. She smiled in amusement as Holly came in for a cuddle, needing to feel Clare's love and Clare filed away that Holly needed aftercare throughout playing, not just after playing. Clare sat down on the bed with Holly and held her close, looking into Holly's sweet, vulnerable eyes after each kiss of her cheek and forehead.

"Do you want to keep going?" Clare asked and patted Holly to spread her thighs when she nodded yes. Clare placed one hand on Holly's chest, letting her weight drop and pinning Holly to the bed, making her gasp for each breath as she slowly snaked her fingers down to Holly's cunt.

"You'll feel this," Clare said as she spanked Holly's pussy with her full hand-making Holly yelp from behind the gag. Clare rubbed her after each spank and enjoyed feeling Holly get wetter with each hit.

"You like this, don't you baby," Clare asked, coming down hard on Holly's wet pussy. Holly nodded, and Clare could see her trying to push past a limit. Clare spent longer rubbing Holly, made her spanks less painful, and loving smiled down at Holly as she pushed two fingers into her. Clare enjoyed how open Holly's pussy was, how desperate she was to be fucked.

"I'm going to fist you, darling," Clare said and pushed her fist into Holly without further warning. Holly clenched her muscles but was too horny to be able to keep Clare out, and Clare began fisting Holly ever so gently. Holly moaned and tried to escape Clare's reach, only resulting in Clare pumping her harder.

"It looks like you can take it baby girl, Mommy is going to use you tonight. Your pretty body is made for fucking, isn't it Holly?" Clare asked rhetorically, putting some muscle behind each thrust of her fist. Holly just lay there, moaning and panting as cum covered Clare's wrist time after time. She took her hand off Holly's chest, and the sudden fullness of her lungs combined with the heat of the room and the fucking she was taking almost made her pass out. Clare saw her eyes begin to roll back and felt her body go limp and pulled out of her. Clare decided the rope would have to wait and took out the gag and blew out the candles, opened her long wall-length window, and held Holly as she came back down.

"I have never felt something so intense before," Holly said in a slurred haze of exhaustion. Clare kissed her and ran her fingers through her wet hair as the sheer white curtains flew out the window and into the small green space outside her bedroom. Holly asked for water, and Clare took her to the bathroom, holding her as they walked. Clare liked having Holly so dependent on her, and she sat her in the bath as she got her a drink. Clare bathed Holly and watched as Holly worked through her space.

"I'll be gone by morning," Holly said to Clare, wanting to keep Clare's rules. She smiled down at Holly and finished washing her hair as she decided on what she wanted to do with her.

"I'd like you to stay if you'd like that?" Clare asked, and Holly smiled weakly, obviously happy with Clare's response.

Chapter 3

Clare called in sick to work the next day. She wasn't interested in working when she had a perfect baby girl to play with. Holly needed no convincing at all to also call in sick, and the two of them stayed in bed for the better part of the morning. They talked about the night they had had and about themselves in general. Deciding that they would need to eat something before they both starved, Clare took Holly's hand and only let go once she was at her kitchen table.

"How do you like your eggs, baby?" Clare asked Holly, who was sitting naked for Clare's viewing pleasure.

"However really, but I like fried," Holly replied, not fussed on what she was eating, all she knew was that she was starving. After the workout Clare had given her the previous night and having not eaten since lunch the previous day, she was famished. Clare finished making breakfast and put a plate in front of Holly.

"Don't touch it," she instructed as she went out of sight. Holly pouted and waited for Clare to return, being very happy when she did. Clare lifted Holly's arms and pulled down a white t-shirt with small cupcake prints on it. She snapped her fingers to the floor, and Holly jumped off her seat quickly to lie down and enjoyed the softness of Clare's touch as she was diapered.

Clare stood Holly up and buckled thin pink leather ankle and wrist cuffs to her perfect skin, leaving her ankles uncuffed but restricting her wrists.

"I don't want you accidentally stabbing your pretty little mouth with a fork baby girl, Mommy will feed you when you are here," Clare said cutting up Holly's food and feeding her until she was finished.

After breakfast, Holly was taken to Clare's living room floor, where she was kept in her cuffs but allowed to roll around and relax into her little space. Clare did the dishes and washed the sheets before she came out to join Holly.

"Well, well, look what I found little one," Clare said, unclipping Holly's wrist cuffs and letting her reach up to grab the block Clare was holding. Holly giggled, and Clare sat next to her as she opened the bag of blocks she had especially bought for Holly and watched as she played. Clare turned on the TV and sat on the sofa while Holly made tower after tower and giggled every time Clare kicked them down with her foot. As Clare grew tired of playing with Holly, she picked her up and put her on the sofa as well. Clare felt Holly through her diaper, and Holly giggled and playfully pushed Clare's hands away.

"I told you not to mess with Mommy baby girl," Clare said, holding both Holly's hand in hers as she gently slapped Holly's face. Pouting and looking down, Holly let Clare feel her and excitedly cuddled into Clare when she opened her arms and let Holly in. Holly began to suck her thumb as Clare played with her hair as she watched her show and was soon asleep in Clare's arms. Clare noticed how Holly smiled in her sleep and gently stroked her cheek, happy she had taken the day off.

Clare had waited for her to wake up and had then taken Holly into her sewing room and let her pick out which material she would like for a diaper cover. Holly had happily selected a light pink, poly-viscose that was thick, very soft, and extremely fluffy.

"Mommy, this feels nice," Holly said as Clare measured her.

"I bet it does," Clare replied, taking the material and cutting it out along the pattern. Holly played with a jar of buttons Clare had given her and watched as Clare transformed the material into a custom made diaper cover, making Holly feel very special.

"I didn't know you could sew Mommy," Holly said, sitting at Clare's feet. Clare looked down at her and smiled.

"How did you think Mommy could have such lovely clothes that no one could ever find in the stores baby girl?" Clare replied. It was not as though her figure was hard to find clothes for, but Clare always wanted to make sure that the clothes she had fit her body to perfection, and that was too hard to find in stores. She enjoyed altering them herself, adding something, or taking something away. She didn't ever want to run into someone with the same outfit she had on, and she never did. Clare finished sewing the material together and held up her creation.

"Gosh, you are going to look so excitingly vulnerable in this baby," she said, eyeing Holly like prey. Holly giggled and reached up to touch the soft material just as Clare had an idea.

"Do you want to be Mommy's cute little bunny baby girl?" Clare asked, taking out a large white pompom and tickling Holly's cheek with it. Holly nodded and rested her head on Clare's thigh as she attached the fluffy whitetail.

"There, come here and let me see you," Clare said, taking Holly's hand and standing her up. Holly wiggled into the diaper cover, and Clare buried her hands in the fluffy material as she rubbed all over Holly's bottom.

"Wow," Clare said, genuinely impressed with herself and wildly aroused by the sweet girl she had at her disposal.

"Do you like it, Mommy?" Holly asked, turning around in circles to try and see what she looked like.

"Yeah, I do, little girl. I like it very much," Clare replied, still in her daze. She sat back down at her sewing machine and got to work, creating another diaper cover for Holly as well as a light purple onesie in the same material. She made sure to give the onesie a little hole at the back, so Holly's bunny tail on her diaper cover could show through.

Clare spent the better part of the afternoon making Holly's new garments and loved watching Holly potter around the room. She grew tired of playing with the buttons and moved onto the collection of ribbons Clare had been collecting for years.

"You are going to be Mommy's pretty little girl, aren't you Holly," Clare said, finishing off the onesie two hours later.

"Yes, Mommy," Holly said, obediently making Clare's clit throb. *I want to do unspeakable things to you,* Clare thought to herself as she watched Holly.

"Mommy, can I wear it now, please?" Holly asked Clare, who was already nodding. Holly beamed and stroked the front of her new diaper cover, loving how soft and thick it was. She dressed her in her new onesie and turned up the aircon to make sure Holly wasn't too warm.

"You look so cute for Mommy baby girl," Clare said as she took out her phone and began to take photos of Holly.

"No, Mommy," Holly gasped, reaching for the phone and making Clare laugh cruelly.

"Your face isn't in it, I'm not stupid baby," Clare said as she continued to capture Holly in her fluffy purple onesie. Holly pouted and began to suck her thumb, and Clare put her phone away.

"Has the baby had enough? Do you want to go home, sweet girl?" Clare asked Holly, who shook her head and held up a ribbon.

"I want to play Mommy," Holly said, smiling when Clare

took it and tied it in a bow around her wrist.

"Oh, look, who is a pretty baby for Mommy?" Clare said as she began to play with Holly.

Chapter 4

Clare and Holly played for the rest of the night, and at 2 in the morning, Clare drove Holly back home.

"See you at work in a few hours, Mommy?" Holly asked, holding Clare's hand as she pulled up to her apartment. Clare had changed Holly back into her original clothes, but her skirt and panties were beyond ruined. Clare had told Holly that on the weekend, she would take her shopping to buy her replacements much to Holly's delight.

"See you then, baby girl," Clare said, stroking Holly's hair and kissing her goodbye.

It wasn't long before they saw each other again, and Clare shifted in the elevator to get closer to Holly. There were only three other people in the elevator with them, and Holly and Clare were at the back. Clare came behind Holly and reached under the mid-thigh hem of her skirt and toyed with her ass cheeks, predatorily groping her as Holly tried to remain straight-faced.

"Cute satin panties," Clare whispered in Holly's ear, almost making her moan out loud. Clare knew that more people would be on the elevator at the next stop and took her hands away, flattening Holly's skirt. Turning around, Holly quickly and almost silently kissed Clare on the lips before turning around again and acting as though she hadn't been her diapered baby girl for the last 24 hours. Clare looked up and smiled to herself; *I want her*, she thought to herself surprised the office slut turned out to be such a sweet baby girl.

As Clare ate her lunch in her usual spot by herself, she saw Holly and her friends sitting on the far side of the abundant water feature in the middle of the green office space. Clare watched as Holly made jokes and ate her lunch, the way she laughed, and the way she flicked her hair had Clare mesmerized. Holly got up and made her way over to Clare, who was shocked that she would risk her popularity to sit next to her.

"Hi," Holly said, sitting down and continuing to eat her lunch. Clare looked at her expectantly.

"Hi, Mommy," Holly said, trying again. Clare smiled at her and made a face, wondering what Holly was doing there.

"Oh, I saw you sitting here alone and thought you might want company," Holly said, replying to the look Clare had just given her.

"If I wanted company, don't you think I could get it, baby?" Clare asked, making Holly blush.

"I just thought," Holly began to say, stopping as Clare put her hand on her thigh, making her look down.

"It's OK, sorry that was mean. Are you having a nice day?" Clare said, stroking Holly, who giggled back at her and nodded her head.

"Yes, Mommy," Holly said, hushing the word Mommy and making Clare smirk. She liked having this power over Holly.

"Holly, I have something I want to ask you," Clare began to say, stopping to see Holly's reaction. Holly looked back at her, waiting for her to finish.

"I want you to be mine. I have loved the time we've spent together, and I don't mind not whipping your sweet little body, there are other things I've enjoyed doing far more, and I think you'd love to be my sweet little girl," Clare said. She hadn't been nervous until now. Holly thought about it for what seemed like ages, and Clare watched as she finished her lunch before speaking again.

"I think you are too rough for me, I think I need a softer Mommy, Clare," Holly replied, as tears began to form in her eyes.

"Don't get me wrong, I have loved how we've played, but I need more of the soft stuff and less of the hardcore psychological stuff. I'm not a slave; I'm a," Holly said, stopping before she had finished her sentence. Clare smiled and took her hand and stroked it lovingly.

"I know what you are, baby, and I'm sorry I've scared you. I can be soft as well darling, but I understand what you mean. Would you still be interested in playing together if we are at the same event?" Clare asked a little disappointed. Holly nodded and leaned over to hug Clare, who embraced her body fully, almost forgetting where they were.

"You can keep the things I made you, you looked adorable in them," Clare said, kissing Holly's cheek.

"Thank you, Clare," Holly replied, getting up and making her way back to her friends. Clare stayed stilling in her favorite place for the next hour, disregarding the work she knew she had piled up on her desk. As she thought back on their time together, she slowly began to feel herself letting Holly go and decided that working through that process was more important than working through her inbox.

Clare and Holly smiled at each other knowingly every time they passed each other in the corridors, and Holly had defended Clare when her friend had said she was quiet and weird. It was a civil and courteous work relationship they had developed but had not spoken a word to each other since that day two months ago when Holly had called it quits. Clare had gone back to her usual professional manner but was happy to see Holly had handed over the title of office slut to one of her friends. As the night of a new party was drawing near, Clare spent her evenings making a new outfit to wear and was hoping Holly would be there.

"You will not believe how cute she is!" Sophie, Clare's friend, said talking about a girl who she had just seen walk into the house party. Clare loved these types of parties the most, where everyone was there because they knew someone. It was nice to catch up with friends and not have idiots causing a scene.

"Who?" Clare replied as Sophie looked around the room, but Clare saw her first. The whitetail of her diaper cover sent a shiver down Clare's spine as she tried to bury the feelings she had for Holly.

"There," Sophie said excitedly, pointing Holly out to Clare.

"She must have made that herself, clever baby, I haven't seen those online," Sophie said, making Clare smirk.

"Yeah, she must have," Clare replied, not interested in ruining the excitement of her friend. Clare watched as Holly played and spoke with other babies and Mommies how she giggled when they said something funny or how she showed them her toys. Clare wished she hadn't of seen Sophie go over and talk to her, Holly lighting up when Sophie gave her candy.

"Forget it," Clare said as she made her way through the house and out into the back yard. A couple of puppies and their owners were playing and talking as Clare looked down to see a cute puppy with a black collar kneeling in front of her.

"Do you want me to throw this?" She asked the puppy who had dropped a toy at her feet. The puppy yipped, and Clare had half a mind to throw it over the fence to see what the little thing would do but just tossed it down the yard and into the darkness.

"She likes you; she always likes the sad ones," came a voice behind her. Clare turned around to see a woman standing close behind her. She was wearing a leather corset that looked a lot like Clare's, making her irritated instantly.

"I'm not sad," Clare said, making the woman laugh and come to sit down next to her.

"Right, that's why you're sitting out here all alone with that depressive look on your face," the woman replied.

"Fuck off," was all Clare could be bothered to say, making the woman smile.

"Or you could just tell me what happened?" The woman asked. Clare turned to her about to give her a lecture as she saw Holly being viciously backhanded across the face by someone Clare didn't recognize. Getting up, Clare rushed back inside and stood in the crowd of people watching what was happening. Holly was crying, and her hair had been pulled out, a woman was standing over the top of her with a whip she had used on Holly's arms and legs. Holly had rolled up into the fetal position, and the woman was resting her foot on Holly's head.

"Did you think I'd just let you go you, filthy little whore," the stranger was yelling. Clare caught Holly's gaze, but Holly looked back down to the ground, broken.

"I'm the one that took you in when you were fucking nothing, and look at you; you're still fucking nothing. You're pathetic, do you know that?" The woman yelled, kicking Holly.

Clare stepped forward and bent down next to her as the stranger started to push Clare away.

"Do you want to come with me, little one?" Clare asked in a voice that she didn't recognize as her own. Holly nodded and reached out her hand slightly as the woman stepped on it making her scream in pain. Clare stood up and punched the woman square in the face taking her by surprise, making her stagger backward. Clare bent down to pick up Holly's bag and took her sore hand gently in hers.

"Come on, sweetie," Clare said as she helped Holly up and held her close as she walked Holly out of the house. The woman followed them to Clare's car yelling and swearing, no doubt informing the entire neighborhood what kind of person she thought Holly was, doing her best to humiliate her. It worked, and Holly began to cry uncontrollably, and as Clare shut the door on Holly's side, she ducked a punch the stranger threw.

"You'll have to do better than that," Clare said, hitting back and landing the woman on her ass on the sidewalk.

"Who was that?" Clare asked a very shaken Holly who was still in her baby clothes as she was driven out of the suburbs and back into the city.

"My ex," was all Holly said through her tears. Clare held her hand the entire drive back to her house and understood why Holly had broken it off with her. She didn't want that kind of rough play; she was traumatized by it.

"You can stay at mine tonight, and over the weekend if you'd like, I won't try anything I promise, you can trust me," Clare said, making Holly laugh through her tears.

"You must think I'm pathetic Clare; I don't want you to have to worry about me, I called it off, remember?" Holly replied.

"Yeah, I do baby girl, but I kinda want to make sure you're OK and have what you need to get over the shit that just happened so, will you let me look after you?" Clare asked, hoping Holly wouldn't fight her. Holly sighed and rested her head on the seat and looked at Clare.

"I'm really lucky to have you, Clare," Holly replied, bringing Clare's hand up and kissing it. Holly nervously looked around, and Clare could feel her mind ticking over, knowing what she wanted before she even asked.

"Can I call you Mommy again, please?" She added, her voice giving her away as she entered her little space again.

"Of course, baby girl," Clare replied, feeling her heart swell for the first time in years. It was a different kind of domination she was about to have over Holly, and she was surprised at just how excited she was about it.

Clare slowed the car down as they reached her street and looked down at Holly, who was nervous about what she was wearing. Clare got out and took her long coat to Holly's door and unbuckled her seat.

"Here," Clare said softly to Holly as she wrapped her

long coat around her, tying it up tight around her waist.

"Everyone will just think you've got a thick booty," she added, making Holly laugh as she got out of the car, and they made their way to Clare's front door. Clare opened the door, and as she shut the door behind them, Holly took off her coat and hung it on the coat hook. Feeling lost, Holly stood still and waited to be told what she could do. Seeing this, Clare took her hand and led her to the bathroom. She gently took off Holly's shirt, diaper cover, and diaper as the bath filled up with water and tipped in some bath salts before helping Holly into the bath.

"This will help, baby girl, but I think you're still going to bruise," Clare said, taking a washcloth and gently began to wash Holly. Holly just nodded, and she brought her knees to her chin and began to cry again.

"I'm not all those things she said I was, am I?" She asked Clare, who shook her head no.

"She just didn't handle the end very well, actually, how did it end between you two?" Clare asked, pulling Holly's legs down. Holly leaned back and let Clare rub her pussy with the washcloth, and Clare liked how trusting Holly was of her.

"Kinda the same way it did with us, except we had been together for five years. But she just got too rough. I didn't want it anymore, and she wasn't prepared to go back to being soft like it was in the beginning, so I just packed my stuff one day when she was at work and left," Holly explained as Clare washed her hair.

"5 years, wow," Clare stated, impressed with the time frame. She had never had anything last more than three years. Holly nodded and wiped the water from her eyes.

"I'm so embarrassed, I'll never be able to show my face in the scene again," Holly said sadly.

"Oh yes, you will, as if those people there tonight have never had some awful ex do something awful to them. I think they were all anxious about you," Clare replied, making Holly smile slightly.

"Come on, baby girl, let's get you diapered and ready for bed," Clare said, making Holly laugh and touch her phone to see the time.

"But it's only 9 o'clock, Mommy," she replied. Clare thought about what she would have done 3 months ago in response to the same remark and was happy she had changed her response to, "I didn't say anything about going to bed did I, sweetie, just that we would be ready so when you fall asleep in Mommy's arms, you are already in your jammies."
Holly lay down and followed Clare's instructions as she was diapered.

"Lift for Mommy baby girl," Clare said, patting Holly's bottom-up. Holly sucked her thumb, and Clare was excited to replace her thumb with a warm bottle. She dressed Holly in a new onesie she had made her three weeks ago when she was missing her dearly and warmed up some milk in a bottle. Bring it over to the sofa, Clare pulled Holly onto her lap and enjoyed the feeling of the snuggly blankets she had set up on the couch.

"Drink it all up baby girl, Mommy doesn't want your little tummy to be hungry," Clare said, taking Holly's thumb out of her mouth and replacing it with the bottle. Clare fed Holly, and just as she had predicted, Holly eventually fell asleep in her arms.

"What a good sweet little girl," Clare said, taking the bottle from Holly's mouth. She knew Holly was asleep but found herself liking their current dynamic and didn't feel like breaking it. As she held Holly, she gently touched her face where the bruising was ever so slightly coming through and frowned, angry that someone had dared hurt her baby.

"I'm sorry Mommy wasn't there to protect you little one," Clare said to Holly, who she had assumed was asleep. Holly opened her eyes, slowly taking Clare by surprise.

"You are now, Mommy," Holly replied, making Clare kiss her on the sensitive parts of her face.

"I'm not going to let anything like that happen to you again sweetie, do you understand?" Clare asked.

"But I don't want to play rough as we did before, I like this, I like Mommy as Mommy," Holly replied to a nodding Clare.

"I know, and that's what I want to be for you. I'm going to take care of everything, little girl," Clare said, making Holly beam up at her. Clare reached for her bag and took out her pacifier.

"Binky," Holly said as Clare put it in her mouth before continuing to watch a show.

The new work week was fast approaching, and Clare took Holly back to her apartment, going inside for the first time. It was modest and small with just enough space to fit two people comfortably, which surprised Clare. By the way, Holly dressed Clare was sure she would have lived in a luxury apartment or at least had luxury furnishings. But she kept that to herself as she looked around Holly's apartment and smiled at the down to earth family photos on the wall.

"Cute baby," Clare said, holding Holly in front of her while she looked at the photos of graduations and family beach holidays.

"Thanks, I use to live with them, but they don't live around here. I moved," Holly replied. Clare could tell by the sadness in her voice that there was a story there but didn't press. Holly broke the embrace and turned around to face Clare.

"Do you think it'll go down by tomorrow?" She asked, referring to her face. She had done a good job of covering it up with Clare's help, but the slight tinge of blue was still visible under some lights.

"I think you'll be fine in a week sweetie. Mommy can touch it up every day at work though if you'd like?" Clare replied, making Holly gasp. She hadn't thought that Clare would want to continue the dynamic past the weekend. She had just assumed Clare had done the nice thing and that would be that.

"So does that mean?" Holly said excitedly but not wanting to jump the gun.

"Yeah, baby, it means you can call me Mommy all the time again. It also means that we'll have to sort out some agreements and such, but yes, I would happily be your Mommy," Clare replied, almost getting knocked down by Holly, who pounced on her for a hug making Clare laugh as she held her baby.

"Do you like being in my arms?" Clare asked Holly, who nodded and snuggled into her neck. Clare knew that there were things she needed to get done that night, but held Holly for as long as she needed. Feeling her heartbeat on her chest and stroking her hair until Holly pulled away, smiling.

"Yeah, I love it, Mommy," Holly replied.

Chapter 5

"Holly, meet me at our spot at the park baby girl, Mommy has some exciting news," Clare said, leaving Holly a voice message. It had been six weeks since the party incident, and Clare and Holly spent every spare moment they had with each other. They had even begun looking at colors to redo Clare's bedroom because it scared Holly with its dark and sordid vibe. Holly got the message and was waiting for Clare when she arrived at the park bench by the pond. It was late afternoon, and Clare had been in meetings all day, and she cracked her neck as she approached the bench, happy to be outside and feeling the warm sunshine on her face.

"Darling," Clare said, addressing Holly. Holly waited for Clare to sit down and hugged her affectionately.

"Mommy," Holly whispered in Clare's ear, making her pussy instantly wet. Clare moved Holly onto her so that she was leaning against Clare as they looked out over the pond. Ducks had begun to come back to the pond after the winter, and they swam about happily. The breeze picked up the leaves, and it looked like a postcard picture with the water lilies and blue sky, happy walkers, and dogs running to catch balls.

"Mommy has some exciting news to tell you, baby girl. So exciting that we are going to be celebrating," Clare whispered in Holly's ear as she wrapped her arms around the slightly older woman. Looking at them together, it would seem like they were the same age, but that was only because Holly had such youthfulness to her, she was five years older than Clare.

"What is it, Mommy?" Holly replied, turning her head back as far as it would go.

"I've been promoted baby, Mommy has made partner," Clare said, getting flicked in the face by Holly's hair as she spun around in her arms. Clare watched as Holly thought through what that meant. Clare was now not only her Mommy but her boss.

"My gosh, congratulations!" Holly exclaimed a happy smile spread across her face.

"Thank you, baby," Clare said, turning Holly back around and repositioning her again. They watched the ducks, Holly resting her head on Clare's shoulder as the sunset and Clare wondered about how they would celebrate.

"Come on baby girl, Mommy thinks you need a few new things," Clare said as they saw the first star come out. Holly took Clare's hand, and they walked out of the park and towards one of Holly's favorite toy stores.

"I've never been in there wearing this before," Holly said nervously. She looked down at her clothes and then looked back up to Clare, who was amused at her discomfort.

"If anyone asks, I'll say I'm buying something for my

little girl, and you're helping. It's not as though I'd be lying," Clare said, enjoying herself. She stroked Holly's hand as they walked through the store, and Holly picked out three stuffies she loved.

"Just pick two, baby," Clare whispered in her ear and watched as Holly spent the next ten minutes figuring out which one to leave behind. Finally, deciding a purple kitty with a white tail and a big soft duck with orange feet, Clare took them to the counter and paid.

"Do you want to hold the bag, baby girl?" Clare whispered as they walked back out onto the street. Holly nodded, and Clare knew she was in her little space.
"Little space with very grown-up clothes, I need to get you home little one, you look like you've played dress-ups for long enough," Clare said, making Holly blush. On the way home Clare stopped into a store and bought herself a new fragrance and paid of heels she had been eyeing off for weeks.

"They are pretty Mommy," Holly said when the assistant had been dismissed. Clare looked in the mirror, and a life she had dreamed of was reflected. There she was, a successful partner of a top accounting firm, a beautiful baby girl by her side, and more money than she knew what to do with.
Clare held Holly's hand all the way home, both delighted with their purchases as they planned a holiday to the Alps together.

"Will you be Mommy's little snow bunny baby girl?"

Clare asked Holly, who was already nodding. Clare made a mental note to make Holly some warmer onesies so she wouldn't be cold as she turned the key and opened the door to her house.

"Dinner, bath, and bed, Mommy?" Holly asked, repeating the routine Clare had set her on as Clare took off her heels and unzipped her dress.

"Take those off first baby girl," Clare instructed, pointing to Holly's black and gold bra and panties. Holly giggled and took them off before passing them to Clare, who had her hand out expectantly.

"Tonight we are going to do bathies first baby," Clare said, walking to the bathroom followed closely by Holly, who had taken her stuffies out of the bag and was cuddling into them.

"Not for in here, baby. Go put them on Mommy's bed and come back; I'll count to ten," Clare said as Holly turned on the spot and walked very quickly to the bedroom. Clare heard her running to get back in time and enjoyed seeing the rise and fall of her chest as she pretended that she hadn't been running in the house. Clare decided to let her feel the tension of her body gasping for air but being denied it and didn't bother punishing her further for running in the house. Leaving Holly in the bath to play after she was clean, Clare went to put away her things that she had left at the doorway. Walking into the bedroom, she smiled when she saw that Holly had tucked her new toys in bed on her side.

"Cheeky minx," Clare said loud enough for Holly to hear who just giggled in response. She undressed and went back into the bathroom for a shower. Clare watched Holly play in the bath as she showered and enjoyed how the room quickly got steamy. Getting out, Clare dried herself before pulling the plug on Holly's bath, making her pout.

"Don't pull that face at Mommy, you know very well you've had enough time in there," Clare said, patting Holly down and making her giggle and squirm when she dried in between her legs. Clare took Holly to her room and put her in a thick diaper before fitting her into her snuggly fluffy legless onesie.

"I don't want this one, Mommy," Holly said, trying to pull it off. Clare looked at Holly, who cheekily smiled back at her.

"Baby, Mommy isn't in the mood for naughty girls," Clare said, taking Holly's chin in her hand, holding it firmly. Holly couldn't help the wicked gleam of mischief escaping her eyes, and Clare held her gaze, which just made Holly giggle more.

"But Mommy, I don't wanna," Holly said again.

"Why are you fussy for Mommy? Do you want to be spanked? Is that it? Has Mommy not spanked you in a while, and now you want to test me?" Clare asked, pulling Holly to her and turning her around to face the wall. Clare moved her hands over the front of Holly's body, squeezing and pulling on her curves, making her wriggle but unable to escape.

"Does the baby want Mommy's attention, sweetie?"

Clare asked, rubbing Holly over the front of her diaper, making Holly moan and push back against Clare.

"Not tonight, sweetheart," Clare whispered in her ear, making Holly pout again and try to turn around. Clare spanked her and pushed her back against the wall.

"Did Mommy say you could move, baby?" Clare asked, making sure not to hurt Holly too badly. She had thought about fucking her on the teddy again; she had learned that Holly could take much more when she was cuddling the teddy but decided against it. Instead, she went to her cupboard and took out a vibrator and gently put it into Holly's mouth.

"Suck it, little girl, Mommy is going to stick it inside of you, and it'll hurt if it's not wet," Clare said as Holly cautiously licked the toy. Clare watched as Holly licked and kissed it to the top and back down again and smiled as she saw Holly try to deep throat it.

"Good girl, baby," Clare said as Holly forced it down her own throat. Clare had steered away from throat fucking her baby but was impressed to see Holly try it another time as tears ran down her cheeks.

"Don't hurt yourself, little girl, Mommy doesn't want that pretty little throat to be sore," Clare said, making Holly smile and go back to licking it. Taking it out of Holly's reach, Clare reached in between Holly's thighs and unclipping the onesie and rubbed over her diaper.

"Do you where this is going to go?" Clare asked Holly, who was biting her bottom lip nervously. Clare raised an eyebrow and slapped Holly's bottom, making her jump.

"Yes, Mommy, in my pussy," she replied quietly, blushing, and looking down.

"Good girl, are you going to let Mommy put it in?" Clare asked, rubbing Holly's diaper covered pussy.

"Yes, Mommy," Holly replied, trying to suppress a smile. Clare could see the excitement in her eyes.

"Mommy's naughty girl," Clare whispered as she pushed Holly onto her back. Holly spread her legs for Clare as she pulled her diaper to the side.

"Take it, baby," Clare said as she felt Holly tighten her pussy around the thick vibrator. Holly took a breath and relaxed as Clare pushed it in until it reached her hilt.

"There, my naughty little girl is going to cum in her diaper over and over again, baby, and only if you're good will Mommy take it out before bed," Clare said, turning it on and watching as Holly let out a frustrated moan.

"Mommy likes it when you're forced to cum baby girl," Clare said, clipping up the clips on Holly's onesie, dressing her again.

"Be a good girl for me, or I'll make you have it in for work tomorrow," Clare whispered as she played with Holly's nipples. She moved Holly up onto her and reached under her arms to play. Holly just moaned as she rolled her head back and came again. She had lost count and felt her body become exhausted by the orgasms Clare was forcing on her.

"Now that Mommy is your boss at home and work, I can punish you everywhere, can't I?" Clare said, reaching down and pressing on Holly's diaper, making the vibrator buzz hard inside of her.

"Yes, Mommy," Holly breathlessly replied, wondering how much she could keep taking. Clare wrapped her arms around her and held her tight as she was forced to orgasm again and ran her fingers through her hair.

"Good girl. Mommy doesn't like having to punish you, sweetie, but you can't be cheeky with me," Clare said, but Holly didn't hear as she bucked her hips and ground down on her diaper as another orgasm built inside of her.

Chapter 6

"Mommy, I'm wet," Holly said quietly, leaving Clare a voice message. Clare had taken to making Holly wear pull-ups at work, mostly to make sure she wouldn't become too sassy but also because she liked being able to keep her in her little space all the time.

Clare listened to the voice message just as a meeting began and smiled to herself, knowing Holly would have to stay like that until the meeting was over.

"Come to my office, baby," Clare replied to a waiting Holly an hour later. It took Holly no time at all to knock on Clare's office door, and Clare very formally invited Holly inside, locking the door behind her.

"Is Mommy's pretty baby all dirty," Clare asked as she put Holly up on her desk and lifted her dress over her pull up. Holly just nodded and began to suck her thumb as Clare changed her. She had often wondered what would happen if one of them forgot to lock the door, not being able to decide if she would like to be found out or not. Clare stopped when Holly had a fresh pull up on and admired her baby girl. Red heels on her black desk, her pretty pink love heart pull up showing, and her borderline slutty black business dress pulled tight across her breasts. Holly knew Clare liked what she saw and was grateful; the last thing she wanted was for Clare to stop being hers.

"Do you want me to rub it, Mommy?" Holly asked, wanting to please Clare. Clare smiled at her sweet girl's request and shook her head before helping Holly down and adjusting her dress over her pull up.

"No, sweetie, if I let you start, I might never let you stop," Clare said as she kissed Holly and held her close. Holly melted into the kiss and was relaxed in Clare's arms before a knock came on the door. Breaking the embrace and beginning to blush, Holly forced herself quickly back into her adult space and cleared her throat.

"Thank you for passing on that feedback, I'll be making those improvements in my next close," Holly said, making Clare almost laugh as she walked to the door. Opening it, to see one of the interns almost shaking in fear of Clare who eyed them in a way Holly never wanted directed at her.

"For you, Ms Jones," the intern said, almost bowing as he passed her a note and hurried away.

"Why are they so scared of you, Mommy," Holly teased, whispering Mommy and smiling cheekily.

"Because they knew just how mean Mommy can be," Clare replied quietly before going back inside and shutting the door behind her. Clare opened the note. It was a playful message from one of the other partners. *You can take your baby girl on that trip next week, just had it cleared,* Clare read sitting back in her chair and smiling up at the ceiling. Not only could she make the intern's life a living hell, but she had real dirt on one of the other partners who had become very accommodating to her desires and requests. She had discovered that he had been stealing from the company for years to pay for his secret stash of illegal's he had set up out of town. His career and political aspirations would be ruined, not to mention his legitimate family publicly shamed if word of his harem were to be made public knowledge. Clare had known for years, but knowledge is power, and she had kept this little gem until she could cash it in, and that was now.

Clare arrived home before Holly, she had gone out with some friends to a bar and would be back later that night. She had tried to get Clare to go with her, but those women pissed her off at work, she wasn't about to spend her free time with them as well. Opening a bottle of wine, Clare poured herself a glass and went out to the courtyard, admiring the blooming flowers she had planted as she sipped her wine.

She was still relaxing outside when she heard Holly come in. It was earlier than Holly had said she'd be home, and Clare smiled when she saw what Holly was holding.

"Mind if I join?" Holly slightly slurred, and Clare pushed a garden seat out for her to sit in. Holly placed the cupcakes she had bought on the table and gazed lovingly at Clare, who just laughed.

"If I had known you'd be so cute drunk, I'd have had you drinking vodka instead of milk from the bottle," Clare teased as she bit into the cake before indicating to Holly she could have hers.

"I am going to need you to take the next week off work Holly," Clare began to say, using Holly's name it get her attention. It worked, and Holly flicked her head around to see why she was being called by her name and not baby.

"I'm taking you on a trip. You won't have much work to do on it; you're purely there for my benefit," Clare explained, making Holly excited.

"Where are we going? Will we catch a flight? Will there be Champaign?" Holly questioned, her eyes growing wide, happy to be getting treats. Clare just looked at her until she settled back down again and continued to eat her cupcake, slightly put out that her questions weren't answered straight away.

"We are going to Sydney, Australia, so yes, of course, we are flying. Mommy is going business class, but you are going economy," Clare began to say, enjoying her white lie of Holly having to go economy and watching her face try not to give away she was extremely disappointed with the plan. Satisfied that Holly didn't complain, Clare continued.

"I'm joking as if I'd make you do that, of course, you're coming with me on business class, how else will I make sure you're a good girl and not being a brat to the hostesses?" Clare said as Holly sat back up, feeling at peace with the world again.

"Mommy has to work during the day, but after work, we can play, and you can show me the places you visited in the day time. We are staying a day longer because I want to see some things, and you can go shopping with my card as well," Clare said, making Holly jump up and dance around the courtyard.

"I love you, Mommy," Holly said happily.

"You love Mommy's money, you little brat," Clare replied, making Holly stop and look at her puzzlingly.

"I love that too, but Mommy, don't you know I love you?" Holly said in her serious little voice. Clare shook her head, and it almost brought Holly to tears.

"Haven't I showed you how much I love you, Mommy?" Holly said, coming over to her and sitting on Clare's lap. Clare bounced her off and pointed to the floor. Holly looked on the concrete floor and knew it would be cold, it had been dark for hours now, and she shivered as she sat feeling the coldness in her bones instantly.

"Show me how much you love me. I want you to make me dinner, run me a bath and be a big girl tonight. Mommy doesn't want to have to do a thing, baby," Clare said, pointing her shoe at Holly, who began to take it off.

"Good, and the other one," Clare said as Holly obediently followed her instructions. Clare took Holly back inside and pointed to the bathroom.

"What did I just say?" Clare said as Holly remembered and quickly walked to the bathroom, making Clare smile when she heard the water being turned on. Clare walked into the kitchen and poured herself another wine before walking into the bathroom to see Holly standing proudly beside the bath she had just ran. She had turned on candles and put rose bath salts in the water, making the room smell divine.

"Undress me, baby," Clare said as she sipped wine while Holly slowly pulled off Clare's work trousers and panties. She reached up and gently unbuttoned Clare's blouse buttons, and the silk material slipped off her shoulders and landed on the floor behind her. Holly smiled, seeing Clare's full breasts curve at the top of her bra and forced herself not to kiss her as she unclasped it. Meeting Clare's sharp gaze, Holly giggled and tilted her head down, excited to be serving this powerful woman.

"Pick that all up and put it in the wash. Then come back here with my pajamas baby," Clare instructed as she sank into the steamy water. She let Holly wait at the door for her and made her watch as she enjoyed her bath, the hot water relaxing her muscles, the bath salts adding to the sensuality of it all.

"You may come in now, Holly," Clare said and pointed to her towel. Holly took it and passed it to Clare, who shook her head and raised an eyebrow.

"Dry me, baby," Clare lovingly said as Holly realized

what she wanted. Holly made sure not to spend too much time rubbing Clare's breasts or ass and was sure not to rub her too hard against her pussy being very aware this was not the time to tease Clare.

"Good girl," Clare said as Holly handed her her pajamas and dressed her without having to be told. Holly wondered when she would be allowed to get clean after the work-day, but her thoughts were cut short by Clare's hand slapping her ass.

"Not right now, obviously," Clare said as though reading her mind.

Holly went to the kitchen and began making dinner. Clare knew it would be nothing fancy, Holly was a terrible cook, but it was the intent behind her cooking that Clare wanted tonight. Holly had settled on an Italian shrimp dish, and the house smelt alive with flavor by the time it was finished making Clare very impressed.

"You've been holding out on me," Clare said, wrapping her arms around Holly's waist, not being able to resist pushing into her spank-able ass.

"I just googled," Holly replied, not wanting Clare to think she was only so clever because she wanted a reward. Clare settled at the kitchen table and made Holly watch as she ate, very aware Holly's dinner was going cold. Usually, Clare would let Holly eat with her, but not tonight, tonight Clare wanted to make sure Holly knew who was in charge. Finishing her meal, Clare nodded to Holly, who began to eat, and Clare watched as she tried not to complain that her dinner was cold. Deciding she had had enough of that, Clare got up and took Holly's plate away. Holly, who would have usually complained one way or another, just sat there and excepted her fate, but was delighted when she saw Clare come back with a plate of hot dinner for her.

"I'm not that mean baby girl," Clare said, kissing Holly's forehead and accepting a hug from Holly, who gave it almost involuntarily.

"Thank you, Mommy," Holly replied as she ate happily. After dinner, Holly tidied and washed up while Clare listened to music and flicked through social media. She looked at pictures of Australia and was surprised she had never been. Holly came to kneel in front of her, making Clare particularly delighted, and she let Holly stay there as she ran her fingers through her hair lovingly.

"I want you to make a list of all the things you want to see, baby girl," Clare said to Holly, who got up and went to find her phone. Clare let Holly on the sofa, and they cuddled while they planned their trip.

"Let's go to see all the big things on a bus tour, so we don't get lost. We can see the Opera house and the bridge; they have some amazing looking cafes. I wish we had places that looked like this," Holly said excitedly, showing Clare the photos she had found. Clare took note and began to write down all the ideas Holly had knowing that this would go late into the night.

Chapter 7

Clare could see that Holly would be a brat the next day the minute she laid eyes on her. It wasn't that Holly was doing anything particularly bratty, it was that she wasn't doing anything in particular at all. Clare listened as Holly quite effectively cleared her morning schedule being delegating almost everything to the interns she had taken from another floor and was happily twirling around on her chair as Clare left her office and walked by.

"Are you right there, miss?" Clare asked her stopping her chair with her thigh.

"Yes thank you, Ms. Jones, can I do something for you," Holly replied as Clare walked away, making her turn her head back and look over her shoulder in playful disbelief on her way to a new meeting.

My Mommy's the boss, and I can do whatever the fuck I want, she thought to herself as she strutted through the office. Clare noticed her continued air of superiority as she waltzed up and down the corridor.

"Holly," Clare said, coming out of her office to catch her on one of her model-like corridor catwalks.

"Yes, Ms. Jones," Holly innocently replied, making Clare roll her eyes and keep her door open as she walked back into the office.

"Will you settle down Holly," Clare said, sitting in her chair as Holly closed the door behind them and slunk down in one of Clare's chairs.

"What am I doing, Mommy?" Holly replied, looking at Clare like she was ready to challenge her.

"Get over here," Clare said, patting her lap, delighting Holly, who eagerly jumped up. Clare bent her over her lap and turned her chair to face the window behind her desk. She was hoping someone could see as she spanked her naughty girl's ass, her heels kicking up as she tried to escape.

"Do you need a little reminder, Holly," Clare asked. Holly was sure that Clare couldn't possibly mean what Holly thought she meant but was grounded hard and fast as she felt the tip of a butt plug pressing into her pull up.

"Mommy is going to remind you what slutty little office dolls get when they are too cheeky," Clare said, pulling the pull up to the side and forcing the butt plug into Holly's mouth.

"Get it wet darling, or it'll hurt like a bitch," Clare said, fucking Holly's mouth until she was satisfied. Slowly pushing it past her ass cheeks, Clare forced it into a resisting Holly, enjoying the struggle she put up.

"Fighting Mommy just makes me wet baby are you trying to turn Mommy on so you get to fuck me?" Clare whispered in her ear as she stood her up, smiling as Holly winced as the plug adjusted inside of her.

"I'll enjoy watching you sway those little slutty hips of yours now you've got that big toy filling you up," Clare said, pressing her fingers into Holly's ass over her work dress before dismissing her.

For the rest of the day, Holly was reminded that she was Clare's, and Clare was happy to see her humility return by the afternoon. Taking a break, they strolled through their favorite park and talked about their soon to be taken trip.

"You know, I've never been happier with anyone else," Holly said as she linked her arm in Clare's.

"I don't doubt that I am the best," Clare playfully replied, making Holly laugh.

"No, I'm serious. You always seem to know what I need, and I love that," Holly said, stopping and looking Clare dead in the eye.

"I love you, Mommy," Holly said, making herself blush. Clare pulled her in and held her tight as a warm breeze blew around them.

"I could stay here forever, baby girl," Clare said as she began to stroke her hair, mildly aware that people could very well be watching. *It must look so out of place, two women dressed in power outfits holding each other so tenderly*, Clare thought quickly, disregarding her care of anyone else but Holly.

"You can take that out when we get back, baby girl,"

Clare whispered in Holly's ear, kissing her on her cheek.

"Thank you, Mommy," Holly replied happily.

Clare waited for Holly to finish the work she was doing at the end of the day. She had already worked two hours after everyone else had gone home, and Clare wondered what on earth was taking so long.

"Holly, get an intern to do it tomorrow, it really shouldn't be taking you so long," Clare said, annoyed she was still at work. Holly typed furiously as Clare rushed her and happily swung around on her chair as she finished.

"Done!" Holly said triumphantly as she hit enter and sent the work to Clare for proofing.

"Good, let's go," Clare said impatiently as she began to walk down the corridor to the marble lobby. Holly quickly walked behind her but stopped when she reached the lobby; she knew that the cleaners would be polishing the floors, and they were always slippery when they did that. Clare turned around to see where Holly was just as she made her way across the floor to take hold of Clare's extended hand. Reaching out to take her hand, Holly felt her heel give way and slip from underneath her making her fall. Clare heard the crunch of Holly's ankle as she hit the floor, and Holly yelled in pain and gripped her ankle with both hands as she began to cry. Clare dropped to her knees and held Holly trying to soothe her, and the cleaning staff stopped to come and see what had happened.

"Can you ring an ambulance please," Clare said through her teeth, trying not to rip the cleaner's heads off. They scurried away, and Clare whispered to Holly, who she could tell was in a great deal of pain.

"Mommy's got you, little girl, you're going to be alright, I'm here, we will get you all better soon baby," Clare said lovingly, wanting Holly to stop crying. After what felt like hours, the ambulance pulled up, and Holly reached for Clare as she was stretched away.

"I'll be right behind you, alright," Clare said as she saw Holly try to be brave as she nodded her head and began to cry again.

Clare ran into the hospital just in time to see Holly being taken to get her ankle X-rayed and held Holly's hand.

"Hi sweets," Clare said, stroking Holly's forehead.

"It's OK, Ma'am, she'll be fine, she's a big girl," the nurse said as she pushed Holly through the doors, stopping Clare.

"No, she's not," Clare whispered to herself as she longingly looked through the windows of the door, watching Holly be taken into one of the rooms.

Clare waited for an hour before she saw Holly coming down the hallway on crutches. Clare was relieved to see her giggling and smiling with a nurse who carried her heel in a bag.

"Well, don't you look interesting," Clare said, seeing

Holly in her business dress and heel on crutches with one foot plastered up.

"It feels so funny," Holly giggled back, making Clare pull a face and look at the nurse before she took Holly's shoe.

"Pain killers," the nurse replied.

"She'll come off them in a few hours and then just over the counter pain killers should do the trick. She's broken part of her ankle bone if you see here," the nurse explained, showing Clare the X-ray. Clare listened to the care instructions and made an appointment to come back and get the cast taken off as well as the ankle rehab methods before they left the hospital.

"Mommy, I was so scared. I asked for the pink cast; I hope you don't mind," Holly asked as Clare helped her into the car.

"I don't mind at all; you look so cute!" Clare said before shutting Holly's door and beginning to drive away.

"It hurts, Mommy. It hurts so much I think I want to start crying and never stop," Holly said dramatically touching her cast. Clare looked at her with an expression that made Holly laugh and was happy they were able to deal with her broken ankle so quickly and efficiently.

"I bet it does baby; I think it'll hurt for a little while yet. But Mommy will take you home and take real good care of you. I won't even make you do the dishes tonight, little one," Clare replied.

"Take the next few days of work, I'll stay home and look after you baby," Clare said, reaching out to hold Holly's hand.

Chapter 8

"This is awesome, I never want to go back to work," Holly said as Clare handed her a bowl of popcorn as they started to watch the second movie of the day. Clare looked at Holly, who just giggled.

"But then, we wouldn't have this great life, baby," Clare replied.

"You can go to work, Mommy, but I could stay home and do this all day every day," Holly explained, making Clare laugh and throw a stuffie at her. This was Holly's second day out of four that she was going to be staying at home for, and Clare was already ready to go back to work.

"That sounds like a very boring life, little one," Clare said, pulling Holly between her thighs and cuddling her. Clare loved feeling Holly in her lap like this, pressing her tits into her back, reaching around to play with her.

"But I could color all day!" Holly said, trying to sound convincing. Clare looked at her, and Holly leaned back into Clare and rested her head on Clare's chest.

"I love you, Holly," Clare said, holding her tight. It was the first time Clare had said it, and the words came out like butter. Holly smiled.

"I know Mommy," she replied contentedly, taking Clare's

hand to her lips and kissing it.

After the movie, Clare took Holly to her room, and she laid her down on the bed.

"Are we going to play naughty games, Mommy?" Holly asked, disappointed when Clare laughed and shook her head.

"No, baby, we are not. We are going to go shopping," Clare replied, taking her tablet out and connecting it to the TV that was mounted on the wall.

"What?!" Holly exclaimed when what she thought was a mirror turned out to be a TV.

"Pretty cool, huh," Clare replied happily. She could still impress Holly.

"Yeah, really," Holly said, unable to form a proper sentence.

"So, come here and cuddle with Mommy while we go shopping," Clare said. Holly hurried over to her and pushed her face into Clare's soft breast.

"I like this, Mommy," Holly said before Clare put a pacifier in her mouth.

"Shh baby have binky," Clare said, typing in her and Holly's favorite stores.

"I like that I don't have to talk to anyone," Holly said. Clare looked down.

"Holly all you've done is talk baby," Clare said, amused at her joke. Holly pouted playfully and went back to sucking her binky.

Clare bought Holly two new sets of dinnerware. One was a lion theme and the other an owl theme with pinks and purples that made Holly clap her hands excitedly. Holly picked out which socks she would like, selecting pink and white striped thigh highs and a pair which had bunny ears at the tops. Clare passed the tablet to Holly, who went to town selecting an array of new crayons, felt tips, and three coloring books that came with stickers.

"Can I take these to Australia, Mommy?" Holly asked as she selected her fifth stuffie. Clare took the tablet and removed one of the stuffies and clicked on a new tab for Holly to search through before handing it back to her.

"I don't see why not. Hopefully, everything comes on time," Clare replied, watching as Holly added almost everything pink to the cart.

"Are you paying for this, Mommy?" Holly asked, suddenly aware that she would scale her selection right back if she had to pay for everything. Clare playfully thought making Holly bounce on the bed to hurry her up sweetly before Clare took the tablet and had a look at what she had chosen for herself.

"Well, you don't need these. And I don't want you having that just yet. But I'll pay for these things baby girl as if Mommy was going to make you buy your things. Your money is for important things, like candy," Clare replied, causing Holly to clap her hands happily.

"I should break my ankle all the time!" Holly exclaimed as Clare settled her down for a nap.

"No, don't you dare try to hurt yourself," Clare said seriously, making Holly look down at her feet.

"I did, you know," she quietly said to Clare, who was putting the tablet down after paying just over a thousand dollars for Holly's ten-minute shopping spree.

"You did what, baby?" Clare replied, not quite knowing what Holly was talking about.

"I did hurt myself," Holly explained. Clare looked at her ankle.

"Yeah, I know, I was there, baby," Clare said, beginning to feel like she had missed something.

"No, Mommy. I hurt myself before you. That's why my side is all inked up, I use to cut there," Holly said hoping that Clare would still love her. To her surprise, Clare got to her knees and pulled Holly's princess t-shirt off, exposing Holly's beautiful side torso piece.

"Show Mommy baby girl," Clare said lovingly. Holly took Clare's fingers and traced them lightly over the scars she had slashed into her little body, ashamed of who she was and what she had been through. Clare stopped at each new scar and kissed it gently, giving Holly all her love.

"I'm sorry you felt like you had to do that baby girl. Was

that when you were with your ex, the one from the party?" Clare asked, pulling her in and holding her. Clare took the blanket that was at the end of the bed and wrapped it around both of them, feeling Holly snuggle under with her.

"No, it was even before her. I got busted having diapers when I use to live at home. They didn't understand; they thought I was weird and sick and dangerous. I guess I believe that too for a while. Like, I was so ashamed to be who I am, to need what I need, and to want who I want, and I didn't think anyone would love me when they found out my real truth. I didn't know how to process it, so I punished myself because that was what everyone around me was doing, as well. I got kicked out of home and lived on the streets for a while. I didn't have anywhere to go, so when Sharon, my ex, took me in, I let her do whatever she wanted with me because at least I could be in diapers and stuff. It took so long to figure out that she was not a Mommy, just an abusive, power-hungry person, and it took even longer to leave her. I felt like I would never find another person who would want me. She would say things like, I'm the only one who knows you, and I'm the only one who will ever love you, it made me stay with her longer than I really should have. I didn't know where I was meant to go if I was to leave her. But when I did, when I found out that there's this massive scene with huge numbers of people who do get this and don't find it weird, it was like breathing for the first time. That's when I got this job and got the tat over my scars to show where I'd been and where I was going, that I survived the hard times," Holly explained. Clare was dumbfounded, so she stayed holding Holly for the longest time before speaking.

"I'm so proud of you, baby girl," Clare said when she finally spoke, which made Holly burst into tears with relief.

"You're safe with Mommy now, and there's nothing you could do that would make me think you are weird. You are my little girl and Mommy is so happy to have you," Clare added, making Holly look up at her with tear-filled eyes.

"So, you don't want to leave me?" Holly said through her tears. Clare pulled her into her and wrapped the blanket around them tighter.

"Not darling, my little warrior baby," Clare said as she rocked Holly in her arms until she stopped crying.

Chapter 9

Clare had decided it was time for Holly to move in and was relieved when Holly had agreed so readily. However, moving weekend turned into, renovate Clare's house weekend as Holly came with a list of things she wanted either changed or rearranged.

"Mommy, it won't take that long, I promise," Holly said as Clare drove them to the hardware store.

"Read that list out to me again," Clare instructed. She was mildly amused. She was going along with this.

"Mommy, I'm too little to read," Holly said as Clare looked at her.

"Well, if you're too little to read, you're too little to have an opinion about what Mommy's house should look like," Clare replied.

"The shower taps in the bathroom and sink. They need to be more modern and easier to use," Holly began without batting an eyelid making Clare smirk and laugh to herself.

"The kitchen cupboards need to be more modern and so does the paint; I'm thinking of ceiling white. I'd really like new rugs for the floors, in like, pink and maybe we could even get new linen for the bed, yours is scary," Holly said as Clare made a mental list.

"And we should get some duct tape for the baby, so I can tape her mouth shut when she talks too much," Clare teased, making Holly gasp.

"We can get everything ordered today, but I want a man to come out and fix everything up for us, I'm not about to play builders with you," Clare said taking Holly's hand and leading her around the store.

"Maybe it's a lady, not a man," Holly said adamantly.

"I don't care who it is. All I'm saying is that I'm not doing any of it so it won't get done today Holly," Clare said, not as amused as Holly was by her political correctness.

"We could get hard hats," Holly said, walking over to the protective gear section and trying one on. Clare was about to dismiss it, but looking at how cute Holly looked, she went over and tied a tool belt to her waist.

"Take it off, you're turning Mommy on," Clare whispered in Holly's ear.

"I said take it off, not put it back," Clare said, grabbing the tool belt and hard hat Holly was about to put back and placing it in the trolley. Holly clapped her hands in delight.

"Do you need one?" She asked Clare, who just scoffed at her.

"No, because you're going to be my little worker, and I'm going to bend you over my workbench and fuck you until the cupboards aren't the only thing that's broken," Clare replied confidently, excited to get Holly home.

"Well, we can't because today's the day I get my cast off my ankle, and the doctor said I couldn't put any serious weight on it," Holly replied, trying to have all the control. Clare just rolled her eyes.

"Then you can be on your back, my little slut," she said as she spanked Holly with an offcut piece of wood as they made their way around the store.

After the store they did, go to get Holly's cast off and were told not to do any strenuous exercise. Clare bit her lip to try and stop herself from getting turned on as the doctor lifted Holly on the table.

"Lollipop?" She asked, offering Clare and Holly the jar. They looked at each other, making the doctor laugh.

"Everyone is a kid at the doctor's," she said, making Clare raise an eyebrow as she took a red one. Holly chose a yellow and happily sucked as her cast was taken off.

"Will I be able to wear heels soon," Holly asked, she had not enjoyed being off-balance with only wearing one heel. The doctor looked at her like she had lost her mind.

"You broke your ankle Holly," she said plainly.

"Yes," Holly replied bluntly, and Clare enjoyed the show sucking on her lollipop. She liked watching Holly be inspected by another woman who was clearly in charge of the situation. She liked it, even more, seeing Holly disciplined by her.

"No, you are not allowed to wear heels for a good two months to make sure that everything heels properly. Don't even think about it, Holly," the doctor replied. Something in the doctor's voice gave her away, and Clare knew where she had seen her before. She thought that she must have had seen her last time they were here, but it was before that.

"Puppy owner," Clare said, making the woman turn around in surprise.

"I saw you at a party Sophie was hosting, you have a sweet puppy, a girl, you asked me why I was so depressive looking," Clare explained, making the woman laugh.

"Wow, yes, OK, and this is the girl you bailed on our conversation for?" The doctor replied. Holly looked at Clare and looked at the doctor, realizing it was better to stay quiet.

"Yeah, this would be her," Clare said, running her fingers through Holly's hair, comfortable to show her affection.

"Well, she looks worth it," the doctor replied, gently slapping Holly's left cheek a few times before turning back to Clare.

"There's a party tonight, if you and yours want to come, we'd love to have you," the doctor said inviting Clare who just smiled and laughed.

"Oh no, she's my baby girl, not my pup, but thanks," Clare said as the doctor shrugged her shoulder.

"If you ever get one, hit me up," the doctor said as Clare and Holly left the hospital.

"Mommy, I don' like her, she would be so mean I can tell," Holly said the minute they were both in the car.

"Yeah, she might be, but we will never know, so don't stress about it, baby," Clare said, wanting Holly back in her little space.

They finished making their rounds to the different stores for linen and rugs before eating lunch at a restaurant. When they got home, they moved Clare's flogging cross to the spare room and redecorated Clare's bedroom with the lighter linen and rug.

"It looks like my room is for a five-year-old with these pink sheets and rug," Clare said as Holly set up her stuffies against her pillow.

"Um, yeah," Holly replied, stating the obvious. Clare laughed and went out to the living room, where she had begun to set up a play space for Holly.

"Do you think I need a playpen, Mommy?" Holly asked as Clare set up the 2x5 meter wooden pen in the nook of the living room. Clare had it custom made and painted in Holly's favorite colors, candy pink and purple.

"Yes, I do little one because Mommy doesn't want your toys spread all over the house, and this is the place you're going to play with them in. Look, there's a spot to do reading and coloring in and all the pillows and toys you could ever want," Clare replied as she started to strip Holly.

"Hey, Mommy," Holly said, beginning to fuss.

"Don't baby girl, Mommy is tired, and you're going to be good and have bathies for me while I make dinner. You're going in your fluffy onesie tonight, and when I cuddle you, you'll feel like a little bunny all sweet and soft," Clare said, picking up Holly's clothes and throwing them in the washing basket as she led her to the bathroom.

"And duckie, and giraffe, and a bucket," Holly said, telling Clare what three toys she would like to play with during her bath.

"OH, please, Mommy, baby girl where are your manners?" Clare replied, withholding the toys from Holly.

"Please, Mommy," Holly replied.

"Because I had to tell you, you aren't getting giraffe tonight, maybe tomorrow night, you'll be a good girl, and I won't have to remind you," Clare said, splashing Holly with water.
Clare dried Holly and was happy Holly didn't fight her to put on a diaper like she did most nights. Clare clipped up Holly's onesie and rubbed her all over, loving how the material felt on Holly's body. Holly hadn't crawled much in Clare's house but began to as she followed Clare back into the living room was put in her playpen.

"Are you a sleepy baby tonight, little miss?" Clare asked

Holly, who was watching her in the kitchen from the bed of stuffies she had made for herself. Holly just nodded her head slowly and rubbed her eyes as she rolled over and began to drift off to sleep.

"Not yet, darling," Clare said as she came over with a bowl of pasta and began feeding Holly.

"Mommy, I just want milkies," Holly said, pushing the pasta away.

"You can have milkies after dinner, baby girl, but Mommy needs you to eat this now," Clare said as she spoon-fed Holly another mouthful.

"But it's yuck," Holly said, kicking her foot in a tantrum.

"That's OK, eat it anyway," Clare replied motherly, knowing full well that the dinner was not yuck at all. She knew this was one of Holly's favorite dishes and forced another mouthful into her when she went to speak again.

"I think you're just fussy because you're so sleepy little one, is that it? Did Mommy work you too hard today, baby?" Clare said, giving Holly one more mouthful before she was satisfied she was finished. Holly pouted and nodded her head, not sure if she wanted to be angry or sleep as Clare stepped out of the playpen and went to get her a bottle.

"Here my sooky baby," Clare said, coming back with Holly's blankie and bottle. Holly reached up, and Clare lay down next to her as she drank and snuggled her blankie.

"There's my good little girl," Clare lovingly said, stroking Holly's hair as her eyes grew sleepy.

"Mommy, I'm done," Holly said, passing the bottle back to Clare and rolling over. Clare leaned forward and saw Holly's eyes were already closed.

"Are you falling asleep here tonight, baby girl?" Clare asked Holly, who just nodded and yawned.

"Alright, little one, sweet dreams," Clare said, kissing Holly on her head and going to have a shower herself.

Chapter 10

The day had arrived where they would be flying to Sydney, and Holly was in fine form. Clare had already spanked her ass red and made her put back one stuffie she had packed.

"Do not keep testing me baby girl, Mommy will have no trouble diapering you on the plane if you keep this up," Clare said. She wasn't joking either, the thought of Holly having a diaper on in public made her excited, and she had been waiting for the opportunity to arise. Clare wondered why Holly was acting up today. *Is she nervous about flying? Is she over-excited because it's a new experience? Or is she just being a little brat because she wants all my attention?* Clare asked herself as she grabbed Holly by the arm and forced a pacifier into her mouth.

"You'll keep it in young lady," Clare ordered, making Holly's demeanor change instantly as a soft moan escaped her throat as she felt the words hit her clit. Sucking her paci, she reached for Clare, who reluctantly held her.

"Are you excited or nervous little one?" Clare said, patting Holly's bottom gently. She was aware that her ass would be sore for a few hours after the almost flogging she had dished out this morning. Holly nodded to excited, and Clare rolled her eyes.

"Then don't mess it up by being so naughty for Mommy,"

Clare replied, taking their bags and heading out the door to the waiting taxi.

They made their way through the airport and checked in their luggage. Holly constantly asked for candy from the vending machines, which Clare continuously refused before boarding the plane and finding their seats.

"This is nice," Holly said as she sat down and began fiddling with everything she could get her hands on. Clare looked over to her and knew that Holly couldn't calm herself down, so she took her hand and held it tight as the plane took off.
Grateful when it was finally time to sleep, Clare put Holly's seat down and tucked her in. The flight attendant who was to take care of them for the duration of their flight noticed the very clear power distinction and came up next to Clare.

"Please forgive me if I am overstepping, but would your baby like a coloring in set?" She asked Clare in a hushed tone. There was only one other person sitting in business class, and they were at the front, Clare and Holly had been sat at the back, and Clare was sure he wouldn't be able to hear anything. Clare looked at the flight attendant and smiled as they exchanged knowing looks.

"That would be wonderful thank you," Clare replied, happy to have their dynamic so open. Holly sat up and looked from Clare to the flight attendant and back to Clare when the flight attendant, who introduced herself as Jenny, came up to Holly and gave her the coloring-in set.

"Aren't you going to thank the nice lady baby girl?" Clare said, making Holly blush.

"Thank you," she said, looking down, and Jenny smiled at her kindly before disappearing behind a curtain.

"Mommy," Holly said, alarmed at what had just happened. Dismissing her, Clare took out the colors.

"Draw Mommy a picture, baby," she said as Holly got to work almost immediately.

Soon time passed before Clare saw Jenny again. This time she passed Clare a wine and Holly a juice box and told Holly what a great picture she had drawn. Holly beamed, and Jenny helped her open her juice box.

"I've got a little one too," Jenny explained, talking to Clare. Clare enjoyed listening to Jenny's Australian accent and noted that it wasn't like those bush accents she had heard on the TV.

"Oh, I'm from the city, where, the more British you sound, the higher class you are, and the more respect you get. But that's more of an Australian secret. I'm happy I don't have the typical come to mind accent that is portrayed over the world. It's hideous," Jenny said, making Clare laugh as Holly finished her juice and handed it to Clare.

"Oh, I can take that for you," Jenny said, holding her

hand out to Holly.

"No," Holly said, making Clare instantly mad.

"Holly, that's not what we say too nice people," Clare said as Holly passed her juice box to Clare. Clare passed the container to Jenny and decided it was time for Holly to be humiliated.

"I'm just going to teach her a lesson, would you like to watch?" Clare asked Jenny, who smiled eagerly.

"Very much so," Jenny replied as she crossed her arms and bit her bottom lip as Clare buckled a pacifier gag over a silently struggling Holly. Clare took the blanket off of Holly, which made her cold and reached into her bag for a diaper. Holly's heart skipped a beat as she saw the diaper Clare was holding and began to blush as Jenny moved to stand behind her.

"You can take off her panties if you like," Clare offered Jenny, who gladly moved to stand over Holly. Clare had laid her down in her seat, and Jenny, with Clare's approval, grabbed at Holly's thighs to lift her taking her panties off.

"You have a sweet one, but you're right, she is naughty," Jenny said, handing Holly's panties to Clare. Clare threw them forcefully onto Holly, who pouted and looked annoyed as she was diapered in front of Jenny. Clare parted her pussy lips and teased her before powdering her and fastening the diaper on tight, its thick pad forcing Holly's thighs apart.

"This is what naughty girls get," Clare said, pulling

Holly's pajama pants back up and rubbing her hands over her diaper. Jenny joined in, and Holly wriggled as she was teased and toyed with.

"Does she have a pacifier? In Australia, we called them dummy's," Jenny explained as Clare passed her Holly's paci.

"Is that because they are for cute little dumb babies who aren't good for their Mommy?" Clare said, playing with Holly. Jenny laughed.

"I don't know why, we just do," she replied, giggling at the face Holly was pulling. Clare had noticed Jenny's large breasts the moment she had seen her and wondered if they were full of milk. Holly had wondered too because she reached for them as Jenny bent over to put her dummy in her mouth, making Jenny laugh.

"I don't think you're Mommy would like that very much, baby," Jenny said, taking Holly's hands away. Clare thought for a moment. Ordinarily no, she wouldn't have liked it, but she didn't feel threatened by Jenny. She was enjoying babying Holly with her.

"You can, if you'd like, they do look particularly full against your uniform," Clare said to Jenny. She sat down in Clare's chair and pulled Holly onto her lap as she slowly unbuttoned her uniform and let it fall to her waist. Holly nervously touched Jenny as Jenny took out Holly's dummy, and Clare came behind her and took off her bra, exposing her two heavy milk filled breasts. Jenny held one in one hand and pulled Holly's mouth to it with the other, gasping when Holly began to suckle.

"Oh, I needed this. Thank you, baby girl," Jenny said.

"I bet, the pressure must be painful at times," Clare said as she stroked Holly. Holly reached for Clare as she suckled from Jenny, loving the feeling of the two Mommies pressing against her.

"This has turned into a reward rather than punishment, hasn't it baby," Clare whispered in Holly's ear. Holly looked up at her with her usual cheeky grin but shook her head, not wanting it to stop.

"This one now, baby," Jenny said, moving Holly onto her other breast. She could tell Holly was getting full by lazily she began to suckle and she smiled and stroked Holly's cheek.

"They are all the same. My little boy always attacks one tit but takes his time on the other one," Jenny said to Clare, who was rubbing over Holly's diapered pussy.

"Do you have to spend much time away from him? Is the distance hard?" Clare asked.

"Well, he is the pilot, and we fly together. The other stewardesses don't know, and I let him fuck whoever he wants, I have him as my baby. I have a husband at home, and it's hard leaving him, but it's easier on him knowing that I'm not going to fuck my little prince," Jenny explained. Clare loved how open she was with was and was surprised by her story. Holly drank Jenny's milk as the sun began to come up, and Jenny took her off, wiping her mouth clean and pulling her uniform back up.

"We will land in about two hours. I've enjoyed meeting you," Jenny said to Clare as they exchanged social media accounts. Jenny kissed the top of Holly's head and went back to being the perfect stewardess bring them hot buns, and bacon and eggs for breakfast.

"Mommy, can I take this off now, please?" Holly asked as she finished her breakfast. Clare reached over and patted her as she smiled.

"No baby, you'll keep it on until we reach the hotel, then I'll change you, and you'll keep that one on until you're wet," Clare replied, making Holly's mouth gape.

"But Mommy," Holly started to say, stopping when she copped a look Clare usually saved for the interns.
Clare dressed Holly in a baby doll dress and sandals to hide the fact she was wearing a diaper and thanked Jenny again as they left and made their way to the hotel.

"Stay still for Mommy baby, you look so cute in your diapy I want to put it online," Clare said as she took her phone and lifted Holly's skirt.

"Jenny might even like it. This is the one she saw you in today," Clare said, taking photos of Holly as she lay on the hotel bed, making sure to leave her face out.

"Mommy," Holly said, embarrassed to be on display, but Clare just kept clicking.

"I told you not to fuck with Mommy, didn't I Holly," Clare said as she posted the photos online for the world to see Clare's naughty girl.

Who is Tina Moore?

Tina Moore has enjoyed the lifestyle of a Mommy Domme for several years. She began exploring kink and BDSM in her youth and found her love of being a strict Mommy Domme in early 2000. Tina Moore is now an author of many MDLG and ABDL themed novels.

Having enjoyed many years in the kink community, Tina Moore combines these experiences with the sweet and naughty things her baby girl does to bring you tantalizing and salacious stories.

Follow her on:

Author Page on Amazon

Instagram @tinamoore.kdp